Prayers for Mental Clarity

Sammy Cross

Published by Sammy Cross, 2024.

This is a work of fiction. Similarities to real people, places, or events are entirely coincidental.

PRAYERS FOR MENTAL CLARITY

First edition. November 8, 2024.

Copyright © 2024 Sammy Cross.

ISBN: 979-8227389015

Written by Sammy Cross.

Prayers for Mental Clarity

In the midst of life's demands and distractions, our minds can often feel like an overcrowded space, filled with endless lists, worries, and thoughts competing for attention. We search for clarity—seeking a mind that feels as clear and open as a quiet morning, a heart that feels light, and a spirit at ease. Prayers for Mental Clarity is a gentle companion on this journey, offering a space for reflection, calm, and the inner peace we all yearn for.

This book was created with the intention to guide you toward moments of stillness and insight, regardless of the noise of the world around you. Whether you're struggling with indecision, overwhelmed by doubt, feeling the weight of mental fatigue, or simply longing for focus in daily tasks, these prayers are here to help clear the fog and bring you back to a place of centered, quiet strength.

Each prayer in this book touches on a different aspect of clarity, offering pathways to inner peace, focus, resilience, and discernment. Through these words, you'll find gentle encouragement to release what no longer serves you, to embrace the present, and to feel the support of something greater as you navigate life's complexities.

Prayer is not just a means of asking for clarity; it's a powerful act of aligning our hearts and minds with peace and purpose. In these moments of connection, we begin to let go of our anxieties and open ourselves to wisdom, understanding, and true insight.

Wherever you are on your journey, may this book be a source of comfort and guidance, a quiet pause in your day, and a reminder that you are never alone in your pursuit of a clear and peaceful mind. May each prayer bring you closer to a sense of clarity, purpose, and peace.

With an open heart and mind, let us begin.

Letting Go of Distractions

Lord, in this moment, I surrender my busy mind,
Release the hold of thoughts unkind.
Take from me the noise, the chatter and strain,
Replace it with peace, gentle and plain.
Help me let go of worries that linger,
Guide me to calm with Your steady finger.
May my thoughts flow like rivers to the sea,
Leaving stillness, a gift from Thee.
In this quiet, may I hear Your voice,
Among all options, help me choose Your choice.
Clear my mind of distractions deep,
So in Your presence, my soul can keep.
Amen.

Finding Stillness

Dear God, bring stillness to my racing heart,
Quiet each thought, let peace impart.
Clear the clutter, release the strain,
Let my spirit find peace again.
Help me pause, as silence descends,
In Your calm presence, may my worry end.
Grant me clarity, simple and true,
So I can seek and be closer to You.
Let my mind rest, my spirit find ease,
In this place of quiet, help me release.
With every breath, calmness flows,
Into stillness, Your comfort grows.
Amen.

Releasing Mental Clutter

Lord, I come with a mind full of weight,
Help me to slow, to release, and wait.
Let each thought drift like leaves on a stream,
Softening edges, like a gentle dream.
Quiet the chaos, hush the noise,
Fill this space with peace and poise.
Draw me close to rest in You,
Where all things settle, clear, and true.
May distractions melt, like snow in spring,
Grant me the quiet only You can bring.
Help me release what clutters and clings,
To find my peace beneath Your wings.
Amen.

Seeking Divine Clarity

Lord, in the silence, I seek Your face,
Clear the clutter, in this sacred space.
Guide my thoughts to clarity bright,
Help me walk with Your pure light.
Let anxious thoughts be still and fade,
In Your hands, let peace be made.
Draw near to calm my restless mind,
And let my heart true peace find.
Help me trust in Your gentle way,
To clear my thoughts and lead my day.
In You, Lord, let my spirit stay,
In silent peace as I humbly pray.
Amen.

Centring in the Present

God, draw me gently to this place,
Clear my mind with Your holy grace.
Help me see only what's here and now,
To live in present, as You show me how.
Release the past, its weight and pain,
Help me let go, be whole again.
Settle my thoughts, and quiet my soul,
With You beside me, I am whole.
Let me see this moment clear,
Free from worry, doubt, or fear.
In Your light, I feel release,
In Your presence, I find peace.
Amen.

Breathing in Peace

Lord, with each breath, I seek Your grace,
To fill my heart, my mind, this space.
Clear away thoughts that cloud and crowd,
And let my spirit feel unbowed.
Help me breathe in Your peace anew,
To quiet all but thoughts of You.
With each exhale, I release my care,
And trust in You, my silent prayer.
Let stillness come, my worries cease,
In You, my heart can find release.
Grant me the calm that only You give,
In this moment, teach me to live.
Amen.

Freeing My Mind

Dear God, free my mind from ceaseless thought,
Help me let go of all I've brought.
The worries, the plans, the endless schemes,
Clear them all, like fleeting dreams.
Replace with peace, a steady calm,
Wrap me, Lord, in Your healing balm.
As thoughts drift by, let me not cling,
But rest in the stillness that You bring.
Grant me space, pure and clear,
To find my way when You are near.
With an open heart and a peaceful mind,
In You, Lord, my rest I find.
Amen.

A Prayer for Clarity

Lord, light my mind with Your gentle flame,
Clear my thoughts, release my shame.
Let the fog lift, my vision clear,
For I know, Lord, that You are near.
Help me focus on what is true,
And see my purpose, found in You.
Wash away confusion and fear,
So Your wisdom, Lord, is what I hear.
Bring me clarity, a pure insight,
A heart that's steady, calm, and light.
In Your truth, I find release,
In Your presence, perfect peace.
Amen.

Quieting My Inner Storm

God of peace, calm this storm inside,
Let restless thoughts no longer reside.
Speak to my heart, soothe my soul,
Help me let go, make me whole.
Clear my mind of noise and doubt,
Show me what life is truly about.
In Your presence, let me find,
A gentle, focused, peaceful mind.
Hold me close, my worries still,
Align my heart with Your will.
Let me live this moment clear,
With Your guidance ever near.
Amen.

Embracing Present Peace

Holy One, let me embrace the now,
To live in peace, please show me how.
Free me from the fears that pull,
Make my mind calm, pure, and full.
Let me feel Your presence near,
Casting out all stress and fear.
With each breath, bring me grace,
In this still, sacred space.
Grant me clarity to see,
All You have in store for me.
In You, I trust, find my rest,
With a heart and mind so blessed.
Amen.

Embracing Serenity

Lord, calm the waters within my soul,
Where waves of worry take their toll.
Let peace descend, a quiet rain,
Easing each ache, each hidden pain.
Guide my heart to stillness deep,
Where Your gentle presence I may keep.
Help me find the strength to release,
All that steals my sense of peace.
Fill me, Lord, with Your embrace,
Replace my fear with holy grace.
In this quiet, help me know,
Your peace, a river, soft and slow.
Amen.

Finding Rest in You

Dear God, my heart is heavy with care,
Lift my burdens, hear my prayer.
Calm my thoughts, let worry cease,
Wrap me, Lord, in perfect peace.
In the stillness, help me breathe,
As I let my tensions leave.
Fill my heart with gentle light,
Guide me through the dark of night.
In Your peace, I seek my rest,
Knowing, Lord, Your way is best.
Teach me trust, serene and deep,
With You, my soul will safely keep.
Amen.

For Peace Beyond Understanding

God of peace, calm my fears,
Wipe away my hidden tears.
Replace each doubt, each heavy thought,
With the peace Your love has brought.
Help me trust, to let things be,
To feel Your love surrounding me.
In Your arms, my fears decrease,
In Your presence, perfect peace.
Guide my mind, gentle and still,
Align my heart with Your will.
May I rest in Your embrace,
With a soul filled by grace.
Amen.

Releasing My Anxieties

Lord, I surrender my anxious heart,
To You, I give each troubled part.
Help me let go of the fears I keep,
So in Your love, my soul may sleep.
Calm my mind, still my soul,
Make me feel complete and whole.
In the quiet, let me find,
Peace in body, heart, and mind.
Take from me what weighs me down,
Replace with joy, remove my frown.
With each breath, a calm release,
In Your presence, endless peace.
Amen.

Finding Shelter in You

Lord, be my refuge, safe and warm,
Shelter me from life's fierce storm.
Let peace be my lasting guide,
Calming fears that storm inside.
Help me breathe in gentle grace,
Feel Your peace in this holy place.
Take from me the need to strive,
In Your love, I am alive.
Grant me strength to let go of stress,
And find in You a sweet caress.
With Your peace, I am whole,
Calm in body, heart, and soul.
Amen.

A Prayer for Soothing Peace

God, in moments when my heart feels tight,
Send Your peace, a calming light.
Soften my worries, ease my strain,
Help me feel whole again.
With every breath, let fear release,
Filling my spirit with sacred peace.
Take from me the need to rush,
And fill my heart with a gentle hush.
Hold me close, let stillness grow,
In Your calm, help me know,
That peace is found in every prayer,
For You, O Lord, are always there.
Amen.

For Peaceful Thoughts

Lord, I ask for peace of mind,
Free me from thoughts that keep me confined.
Help me quiet every fear,
To know Your peace is always near.
In this silence, still my heart,
Help me from my worries part.
In Your love, I am complete,
Finding peace in Your retreat.
Teach me patience, calm, and grace,
To feel Your peace in this place.
Guide my thoughts to gentle ground,
In Your presence, peace is found.
Amen.

Surrendering to Peace

God, I lay my burdens down,
Let peace replace my anxious frown.
Help me trust, let go of need,
In Your love, plant calm's seed.
Let peace grow within my chest,
And guide my spirit into rest.
As I surrender, make me whole,
Fill me, Lord, in heart and soul.
Hold me steady, soft and sure,
In Your peace, I am secure.
May I feel Your calm unfold,
Gentle, quiet, pure and bold.
Amen.

Finding Calm Amidst Chaos

Lord, in this world's endless rush,
Grant me stillness, a holy hush.
Let chaos fade, and peace increase,
Bring me, Lord, to lasting peace.
Help me pause, and breathe anew,
In every moment, feeling You.
Calm my mind and quiet my heart,
Your perfect peace will never part.
Teach me, Lord, to trust each day,
Letting anxious thoughts drift away.
With You, I find my place to be,
In calm, in peace, eternally.
Amen.

A Prayer for Lasting Calm

Holy One, I seek Your grace,
Calm my spirit, fill this space.
Let peace flow through every thought,
Bringing calm as You have taught.
May each worry lose its hold,
As Your gentle peace unfolds.
Guide my heart to let fear cease,
And find in You eternal peace.
In this quiet, let me know,
Your peace, a calm and steady flow.
In Your presence, all is right,
Calm and peace through day and night.
Amen.

A Prayer for Steady Focus

Lord, my thoughts so often stray,
Help me focus on today.
Guide my mind to what is near,
Make each moment bright and clear.
Remove distractions, still my soul,
Help me achieve what makes me whole.
With steady hands and a heart aligned,
Grant me clarity of mind.
Let me finish what I start,
With strength of will and steady heart.
Your wisdom, Lord, will guide my way,
To stay on track throughout the day.
Amen.

Clearing the Path to Concentration

God, my mind feels scattered and torn,
Help me focus, renew and reform.
Quiet the noise, the endless drift,
Center my thoughts, Your steady gift.
Each task before me, let me embrace,
Working with diligence and grace.
Remove all doubt, clear confusion away,
Help me remain in this moment and stay.
Guide my steps, let me be true,
To finish the work You've called me to do.
With You beside me, I cannot fail,
Keep me steady, strong, and hale.
Amen.

Strength for the Task Ahead

Lord, I feel the pull of delay,
Help me focus, guide my way.
Distractions come from every side,
But in Your wisdom, let me abide.
Grant me strength to push through strife,
To center my efforts and better my life.
Keep my mind sharp, my purpose clear,
With every task, may You be near.
Help me complete what I've begun,
With steady focus until it's done.
In this work, let Your power flow,
That through my effort, Your light will show.
Amen.

Overcoming Procrastination

Dear God, I feel the urge to wait,
To delay the work upon my plate.
Help me move with focus strong,
To act with purpose, where I belong.
Still the doubts that cloud my mind,
Let productivity be what I find.
Help me resist distraction's call,
To finish my tasks, no matter how small.
With You, Lord, I can remain,
Focused, steady, through the strain.
In my work, let my efforts shine,
A reflection of Your design.
Amen.

Concentration Amid Chaos

Lord, the world around me spins,
With endless noise and countless sins.
Help me find a quiet place,
To focus on Your steady grace.
Clear my mind, still my heart,
Help me give each task its start.
Guide me to finish with steady hand,
In Your wisdom, help me stand.
Let interruptions fade away,
Help me focus throughout the day.
With You, Lord, my work is sound,
Focused, clear, and purpose-bound.
Amen.

A Prayer for Mental Clarity

God, my mind feels lost in haze,
Help me see through the mental maze.
Clear the fog, the doubts, the fears,
Make my focus sharp and sincere.
Each task I face, help me complete,
With Your guidance, no task defeat.
Center my mind, keep me aligned,
On the work before me, with peace defined.
Let each thought fall into place,
Organized by Your steady grace.
Help me work with clear intent,
Focused fully, time well spent.
Amen.

Seeking a Focused Heart

Dear Lord, let my heart align,
With tasks ahead, both Yours and mine.
Help me focus on what is good,
To act with care, as I should.
Quiet the chatter that fills my brain,
Replace it with purpose clear and plain.
Each moment, guide my wandering mind,
To leave distractions far behind.
Help me stay on the path You set,
With no delays or time to fret.
With You as my guide, my focus remains,
On work that honours and proclaims Your name.
Amen.

Battling Distraction

Lord, distractions come from every side,
Pulling me from the path You provide.
Help me resist their tempting pull,
And keep my thoughts steady and full.
Grant me the strength to persevere,
To give each moment my focus clear.
Let no task fall to the wayside,
But let me work with You as my guide.
Help me see the task at hand,
With a steady heart and mind to stand.
In my work, let me find delight,
Guided always by Your light.
Amen.

Staying Present in the Moment

God, teach me to stay in the now,
To focus on each moment somehow.
Help me avoid the anxious drift,
And keep my mind on this precious gift.
Let each task hold my intent,
With focus steady, time well spent.
Guide me away from worry's snare,
To act with purpose, calm and care.
In this moment, I find peace,
My scattered thoughts begin to cease.
With You, Lord, I am strong and true,
Focused fully on what I do.
Amen.

A Prayer for Purposeful Focus

Lord, I ask for focus deep,
For strength of mind and peace to keep.
Let my thoughts be clear, not stray,
With diligence to work today.
Help me see each task as light,
A chance to honour, to do what's right.
Remove the urge to pause or stray,
Keep me centered throughout the day.
May my work reflect Your care,
Done with purpose, truth, and prayer.
Help me stay the course, complete,
With every effort, my goals to meet.
Amen.

Seeking Divine Wisdom

Lord, I come with questions deep,
Decisions heavy, thoughts that seep.
Grant me wisdom, clear and bright,
Guide me through the darkest night.
Help me discern what is right and true,
To follow the path that leads to You.
Let my choices reflect Your light,
Shining steady, pure, and bright.
Teach me patience, help me see,
The way that's best, designed by Thee.
Guard my heart, my thoughts refine,
That my decisions align with Thine.
Amen.

For Discernment in Choices

God of wisdom, hear my prayer,
Guide me with Your loving care.
When choices come, complex and vast,
Help me seek the path that lasts.
Still my mind, remove the haze,
Show me the path that earns Your praise.
Grant me courage to choose what's right,
Even when the way is tight.
Help me trust Your steady hand,
To discern what's true, to understand.
With You, Lord, my heart is sure,
In Your wisdom, I'm secure.
Amen.

Choosing the Right Path

Lord, before me lies a maze,
Paths uncertain, filled with haze.
Guide my steps, show me the way,
To walk in truth, not led astray.
Let Your wisdom light my mind,
Helping me to seek and find.
Reveal the road You want me to take,
With choices pure for Your name's sake.
Teach me to listen, to hear Your voice,
In every moment, make me rejoice.
With You, I know I cannot fall,
Your wisdom guides me through it all.
Amen.

A Prayer for Clarity in Decisions

Dear God, decisions weigh on me,
Help me choose what's best for Thee.
May I not be swayed by fear,
But hear Your guidance strong and clear.
Grant me insight, help me know,
The seeds of wisdom You will sow.
Refine my thoughts, remove the doubt,
Help me figure this all out.
Through Your Spirit, show the way,
To live in truth each passing day.
In every choice, may I be wise,
Seeing life through Your holy eyes.
Amen.

For Understanding Beyond My Own

Lord, my wisdom feels so small,
I need Your help, I need it all.
Grant me knowledge from above,
Guided always by Your love.
Teach me to see where I am blind,
To trust in You with heart and mind.
Let every step and choice I make,
Be blessed by wisdom for Your sake.
Guard my heart from foolish pride,
With You, Lord, as my guide.
May Your Spirit always be near,
To lead me forward without fear.
Amen.

Trusting in Your Wisdom

God, I trust in what You know,
Your wisdom far beyond my own.
Help me release my anxious grip,
And lean on You in fellowship.
When I am lost, unsure, afraid,
Help me walk the path You've laid.
Clear my mind of worldly care,
And guide my choices through prayer.
Your ways are true, Your light is clear,
With You, no wrong shall I fear.
Hold me close, in wisdom's embrace,
As I navigate this sacred space.
Amen.

For Courage in Difficult Decisions

Lord, the choices I must face,
Require wisdom, strength, and grace.
Give me courage to do what's right,
Even when it costs the fight.
Grant me discernment, help me see,
The way that honours truth and Thee.
May I resist the urge to stray,
From what is true, from Your way.
Help me act with faith and trust,
To make decisions pure and just.
In every choice, may Your will shine,
So my heart stays forever aligned.
Amen.

Listening for Your Voice

God, I long to hear Your voice,
To guide me in each daily choice.
Speak to my heart, gentle and true,
Show me, Lord, what I must do.
Remove confusion, clear the haze,
Light my path with wisdom's rays.
Help me trust in what You say,
And walk Your path each step of the way.
In moments of doubt, let Your peace stay,
Helping me discern Your holy way.
Guide my mind and still my fear,
Your wisdom, Lord, is always near.
Amen.

Discerning Good from Evil

Lord, in this world of shadow and light,
Help me discern what's wrong and right.
Give me strength to walk the path,
That avoids destruction, avoids wrath.
Let me see with Your holy sight,
To choose the good, to fight the fight.
Protect my heart from deceitful lies,
Help me act as one who is wise.
With each decision, great or small,
May I always hear Your call.
Keep me close, Lord, help me stay,
On the path of truth today.
Amen.

Wisdom for Life's Journey

God of wisdom, walk with me,
Through life's journey, help me see.
Teach me to pause, to seek Your grace,
In every choice, in every place.
When I feel lost, unsure, or torn,
Help me remember why I was born.
Guide me to live in a way that is true,
Honouring always what pleases You.
Grant me wisdom, patient and kind,
A heart that's gentle, a focused mind.
In all I do, let Your will be done,
For Your glory, Holy One.
Amen.

A Prayer for Renewed Strength

Lord, my mind feels heavy and worn,
Weighed down by tasks, my spirit torn.
Grant me rest, a moment to pause,
To find my strength within Your cause.
Restore my focus, clear my thought,
With Your peace, renew what's fraught.
Lift this weight, refresh my soul,
Make me feel steady, calm, and whole.
Help me breathe, let stillness grow,
Infuse me with energy only You bestow.
With Your guidance, my strength is found,
Your love and power know no bound.
Amen.

For Rejuvenation and Energy

Lord, I come with a weary mind,
Seeking strength and peace to find.
In Your presence, may I renew,
A clear and focused path through You.
Lift the fog, the weight of strain,
Restore my joy, remove the pain.
Help me rise from exhaustion's grip,
To find in You my steady ship.
Replenish my thoughts, sharpen my view,
Guide me in all I say and do.
With You, Lord, my energy flows,
And through Your love, my spirit grows.
Amen.

A Prayer for Mental Clarity

God, my thoughts are scattered wide,
Help me find clarity inside.
Calm my mind, bring focus near,
Let me feel Your presence clear.
Take my weariness, make it light,
Infuse me with Your holy might.
Help me see the path ahead,
With sharpness where I once felt dread.
Renew my mind, refresh my heart,
Grant me strength to do my part.
Through You, Lord, my strength is found,
Your peace and power know no bound.
Amen.

Overcoming the Fog of Fatigue

Lord, I feel my mind weighed down,
With heavy thoughts that make me frown.
Send Your light to break this haze,
To renew my mind in joyful ways.
Help me focus, grant me peace,
Let the grip of fatigue release.
In You, Lord, my strength is sure,
Your love and power forever endure.
Help me rise, though tired I feel,
Let Your presence renew and heal.
With every breath, make me whole,
Rejuvenate my weary soul.
Amen.

Restoring Energy and Focus

Lord, I feel so drained today,
Renew my mind, show me the way.
Help me find the strength I need,
To focus, grow, and to succeed.
Infuse my heart with energy bright,
Let Your love restore my sight.
Clear the fog, the mental strain,
Replace it with Your peace again.
In Your hands, I rest my care,
Trusting You are always there.
Guide me forward, keep me strong,
Let Your presence help me along.
Amen.

For Rest and Rejuvenation

God, I feel my strength is low,
Restore my mind, let energy flow.
Bring me rest and peaceful sleep,
A calm so steady, soft, and deep.
Refresh my spirit, renew my soul,
Fill the spaces where I feel the toll.
Help me rise with focus clear,
With Your presence always near.
Grant me energy for this day,
Guide my steps, show the way.
In You, Lord, my strength is new,
Your power sustains in all I do.
Amen.

Lifting the Burden of Weariness

Lord, my mind feels heavy and slow,
I need Your strength to help me grow.
Lift this burden, renew my sight,
Grant me focus, clear and bright.
Take my weariness, make it small,
Restore my energy through it all.
Guide my steps and light my way,
Grant me focus to face this day.
Your peace refreshes, Your love revives,
Through You, Lord, my spirit thrives.
Help me rise with focus keen,
With You, Lord, my path is seen.
Amen.

A Prayer for Mental Refreshment

God, my thoughts feel dull and weak,
I turn to You, Your strength I seek.
Clear my mind, bring focus true,
Help me see my purpose through.
Refresh my heart, renew my care,
Infuse my spirit with strength so rare.
With every breath, help me feel,
Your power to refresh and heal.
Grant me energy, sharp and bright,
Restore my mind to face the fight.
Through You, my strength is restored,
My focus renewed by Your holy Word.
Amen.

Restoring Joy in the Work

Lord, I've lost the joy I knew,
Renew my mind to start anew.
Clear the haze, lift my stress,
Help me work with greater success.
Guide my heart, refresh my soul,
Make my weary spirit whole.
Grant me focus, sharp and kind,
Replenish my body, heart, and mind.
In Your care, I find my way,
Strength renewed for another day.
Your love restores, Your peace sustains,
Through You, Lord, no fatigue remains.
Amen.

For New Strength and Purpose

God, my energy feels so low,
Help me rise and let it show.
Grant me strength, clarity, and peace,
Help my mental strain to cease.
Lift my thoughts to heights anew,
Help me find my focus through You.
With renewed purpose, let me stand,
Guided by Your steady hand.
Through every moment, help me stay,
Focused, strong, throughout the day.
In Your love, I find my fire,
To press ahead and never tire.
Amen.

Releasing Doubts to God

Lord, my heart is filled with doubt,
Help me cast these burdens out.
Show me the truth of who I am,
In Your love, I know I can.
Silence the voice that speaks unkind,
Replace it with Your peace of mind.
Help me trust the gifts You've given,
To walk in purpose, spirit-driven.
Let Your truth dispel my fear,
Remind me, Lord, You're always near.
In Your strength, I will believe,
Your love affirms, Your power relieves.
Amen.

Finding Strength in God's Promise

God, when insecurities arise,
Help me see myself through Your eyes.
When doubts creep in, whisper Your truth,
To remind me of Your unchanging proof.
You made me whole, I am enough,
Even when the road is tough.
Help me stand, both strong and sure,
In Your grace, I am secure.
Erase the lies, replace my fear,
With words of love that draw You near.
With confidence, I'll face each day,
For Your wisdom lights my way.
Amen.

A Prayer to Trust Myself

Lord, I struggle to trust my voice,
Help me believe I've made the right choice.
Guide me to see the gifts You've placed,
In this journey that I've embraced.
When doubt attacks, hold me strong,
Help me know I do belong.
Remind me, Lord, You've called my name,
To walk in purpose without shame.
Fill my heart with courage true,
To act with faith, to follow through.
With You beside me, I can stand,
Confidently led by Your hand.
Amen.

Overcoming the Lies of Insecurity

God, the lies of doubt ring loud,
Help me rise above the crowd.
Let Your truth break through my mind,
And fill me with peace that's kind.
When I feel weak, let me be bold,
To claim the strength Your love has told.
In moments of fear, Your voice I'll hear,
Saying, "Child, I am always near."
Replace my doubts with hope anew,
And courage to see what I must do.
Help me believe in what You see,
A soul beloved and truly free.
Amen.

Embracing My Worth

Lord, I question my own worth,
Remind me of my heavenly birth.
You made me whole, unique, complete,
With gifts and talents none can repeat.
Help me see myself as You do,
Beautiful, capable, steady, and true.
Remove the chains of fear and shame,
Replace them with confidence in Your name.
In every step, let me find,
Your strength and power within my mind.
With You, Lord, I'm enough today,
Lead me forward, show the way.
Amen.

Finding Courage in Fearful Moments

Lord, when fear shakes my core,
Help me remember I'm so much more.
Not defined by failure or shame,
But by the power of Your name.
When insecurity tries to bind,
Replace its grip with peace of mind.
Strengthen my heart, let courage grow,
Through Your truth, let my spirit glow.
Help me take each step with grace,
And see Your light in every place.
With faith in You, my fears are small,
For Your love conquers all.
Amen.

Letting Go of Negative Thoughts

God, my mind is filled with strife,
Help me let go and embrace new life.
Take these thoughts that weigh me down,
Replace them with joy that knows no bound.
Fill my heart with hope and peace,
So doubts and fears will finally cease.
Let Your truth be my guiding star,
To remind me always of who You are.
Help me think with clarity,
With faith and love, setting me free.
In You, I find the strength to stand,
With courage held within Your hand.
Amen.

Trusting in My Abilities

Lord, You've given me all I need,
Help me act with faith and speed.
When self-doubt clouds my view,
Help me trust in what is true.
You have equipped me with each gift,
Let confidence within me lift.
Remind me I am strong and bold,
In Your arms, my worth is told.
With every challenge, I will grow,
Through Your wisdom, I will know.
My abilities come from You, my King,
In Your love, I'll do all things.
Amen.

Quieting the Voice of Doubt

Lord, the voice of doubt is loud,
Pulling me down, dark and proud.
Help me hear Your gentle tone,
That reminds me I'm never alone.
When I falter, when I fear,
Whisper words of courage near.
Help me trust the path I take,
To walk with faith in steps I make.
Quiet the noise of doubt and lies,
Show me truth through Your holy eyes.
In Your strength, I rise above,
Held secure in Your endless love.
Amen.

Building Confidence in Your Love

God, I long to stand with grace,
With confidence to run this race.
When insecurities try to creep,
Guard my mind, let faith run deep.
Fill me with the courage I need,
To follow through with every deed.
Help me stand, firm and strong,
Assured of where I belong.
Your love defines my worth and name,
Replacing fear, erasing shame.
With You, Lord, I'll boldly stand,
Securely held within Your hand.
Amen.

Trusting Inner Wisdom

Lord, You placed wisdom deep inside,
A voice of truth where You reside.
Help me trust this sacred space,
To hear Your whispers of love and grace.
Guide my thoughts, align my heart,
Show me the wisdom You impart.
In moments unclear, let me know,
The path of light where I should go.
Help me trust my inner sense,
With faith in You as my defence.
Through quiet reflection, let me hear,
Your voice of guidance calm and clear.
Amen.

Finding Clarity Within

God, when the world feels loud and wild,
Help me return to the heart of a child.
To trust the stillness You've placed in me,
A sacred source of clarity.
Let my intuition brightly shine,
Guided always by Your design.
Help me discern what's wrong and right,
And follow Your wisdom with delight.
When doubts arise and fears persist,
Remind me of the love I've missed.
In Your presence, I will find,
The answers placed within my mind.
Amen.

Seeking Guidance in Uncertainty

Lord, when the road is hard to see,
Help me trust You dwell in me.
Guide my steps, help me hear,
The inner voice that draws You near.
In every choice, help me discern,
The lessons I am here to learn.
Let my intuition steady my way,
To follow truth throughout each day.
When questions linger, doubts remain,
Help me trust You'll make it plain.
Through the quiet, let me hear,
Your guidance strong, Your presence clear.
Amen.

Aligning with Divine Wisdom

God of wisdom, dwell in my heart,
Help me feel Your sacred part.
Align my mind with what is true,
To follow the path that leads to You.
When I am lost, unsure, afraid,
Help me hear the plans You've laid.
Through intuition, sharp and kind,
Reveal the truth You wish I'd find.
Help me listen, trust, and feel,
The gentle nudge that says You're real.
In every choice, through every task,
Let Your wisdom be all I ask.
Amen.

Embracing Inner Stillness

Lord, in the stillness, help me know,
The inner wisdom You bestow.
When the path ahead feels unclear,
Help me trust You are always near.
Let my heart feel calm and still,
Guided only by Your will.
Show me how to deeply trust,
The quiet voice that says I must.
In moments of doubt, let me find,
The peace that lives within my mind.
With You, I'll never go astray,
For Your guidance lights my way.
Amen.

Trusting My Inner Voice

God, You speak in whispers small,
A gentle nudge, a quiet call.
Help me hear and trust that sound,
The place where wisdom can be found.
When doubts surround and fears arise,
Help me see with steady eyes.
Through intuition, pure and true,
Help me follow what pleases You.
Let me trust what You reveal,
Through inner guidance, help me heal.
In faith and love, I'll boldly go,
With the inner peace You let me know.
Amen.

For Inner Light and Clarity

Lord, let Your light shine within,
Illuminating where to begin.
Through intuition, clear and bright,
Guide my steps with gentle light.
Help me trust my heart to lead,
Where wisdom grows and doubts recede.
Let me hear Your voice so near,
Whispering truth I long to hear.
When choices come, when paths divide,
Help me see where You abide.
Through inner guidance, help me find,
Your will for me, with peace of mind.
Amen.

Navigating with Confidence

Lord, when life feels like a maze,
Guide my steps through winding ways.
Help me trust my heart and mind,
To see the answers You've designed.
In every moment, let me hear,
The inner voice that draws You near.
Help me feel Your steady hand,
Guiding me where I should stand.
Through intuition, strong and true,
Help me act in ways that honour You.
In every choice, through every test,
Let me trust You'll lead me to rest.
Amen.

Hearing God's Whisper

God, Your voice is soft and still,
Yet it guides me with gentle will.
Help me quiet my restless mind,
To hear the wisdom You've designed.
Let intuition rise within,
The place where Your guidance begins.
Help me listen, trust, and see,
The path You've set ahead for me.
When I doubt and second-guess,
Remind me, Lord, of Your caress.
Through inner guidance, help me grow,
With faith in all You let me know.
Amen.

Walking in Intuitive Faith

Lord, let me walk with faith secure,
Through inner wisdom, strong and pure.
Help me trust the voice inside,
The place where You and I abide.
When the road ahead feels steep,
Through intuition, my courage keep.
Help me act with steady grace,
To honour You in every place.
Your Spirit speaks where silence lives,
With wisdom only Your love gives.
Help me trust this sacred guide,
With You, Lord, always at my side.
Amen.

Releasing Regrets to God

Lord, I carry the weight of regret,
Memories I cannot forget.
Take this burden, lift this pain,
Help me see beyond the strain.
Teach me to let the past stay behind,
To trust in Your grace, pure and kind.
Fill my heart with peace today,
Help me release what holds me at bay.
In Your mercy, I am made new,
Forgiven, loved, and guided by You.
Help me move with strength and grace,
And find Your light in every space.
Amen.

Letting Go of the Past

God, I look back and feel the sting,
Of choices past, the hurt they bring.
Help me let go of shame and pain,
To see the lessons, not the strain.
You redeem all broken parts,
Healing wounds within my heart.
Remind me, Lord, I'm not defined,
By my mistakes, but by Your design.
Teach me to live in the here and now,
And trust in You to show me how.
The past is gone, the future bright,
With Your love as my guiding light.
Amen.

Finding Freedom from the Past

Lord, the past feels like a chain,
Holding me captive in its pain.
Break these bonds, set me free,
To live the life You've planned for me.
Help me trust in Your embrace,
To leave behind what I cannot face.
Renew my heart, make me whole,
Cleanse the shadows in my soul.
Each step forward, I take with You,
With a heart that's made brand new.
Let me find in You my rest,
And trust Your plan is always best.
Amen.

A Prayer for New Beginnings

God, I long to start again,
Free from guilt and haunting pain.
Help me release the things I've done,
To see my future in Your Son.
The past no longer has a claim,
For in Your love, I have no shame.
Teach me to forgive myself too,
And trust in all You'll lead me through.
Each day is new, a gift to embrace,
A chance to live in Your sweet grace.
Let my heart be light and free,
With eyes on all You've planned for me.
Amen.

Releasing Painful Memories

Lord, I hold memories sharp and deep,
Wounds that surface when I sleep.
Help me release them into Your care,
To find healing in the love You share.
Let me see beyond the pain,
To where Your grace and mercy reign.
Remind me, Lord, I'm not alone,
For in my heart, You've made Your home.
Replace regret with hope anew,
With joy and peace that come from You.
Help me live in the here and now,
With faith in You to show me how.
Amen.

Letting Go of Shame

God, I feel the weight of shame,
Help me trust in Your holy name.
For in Your love, I am set free,
Forgiven, redeemed, whole in Thee.
Teach me to let the past unwind,
To leave it far, far behind.
Help me focus on what's ahead,
To follow the path that You've led.
With every breath, let shame release,
And in its place, bring perfect peace.
With You, Lord, I am made new,
Each step forward begins with You.
Amen.

Healing from Past Mistakes

Lord, my past feels like a scar,
A reminder of times I strayed so far.
But in Your love, I've been restored,
Made whole again by my risen Lord.
Help me let these memories fade,
Trusting in the progress I've made.
With every step, I'll walk in light,
Leaving behind what isn't right.
Help me forgive myself today,
And live in Your mercy every way.
The past is gone, the future bright,
With You, Lord, as my guiding light.
Amen.

Finding Peace in Forgiveness

God, I've clung to mistakes too long,
Help me see that with You, I am strong.
Forgive my faults, as I forgive too,
Help me embrace a life that's new.
Teach me to release the pain,
To find freedom in Your name.
Help me live with peace of mind,
Leaving all regrets behind.
In Your love, my heart is light,
With You, my future is bright.
Help me trust each step I take,
For in You, Lord, I am remade.
Amen.

A Prayer for Moving Forward

Lord, my past no longer defines,
For in You, I've left it behind.
Help me trust in who I am,
A child of God, redeemed by the Lamb.
Let regrets dissolve and fade,
As I walk in the path You've made.
Help me see the beauty here,
To trust in hope, not live in fear.
Each moment forward is a gift,
To find joy and let my soul lift.
With You, Lord, I am free,
A new creation, whole in Thee.
Amen.

Living Free from the Past

Lord, help me live free today,
Leaving the past in yesterday.
No more regrets, no more shame,
For in You, I have a new name.
Help me focus on what's ahead,
And trust in all that You've said.
Guide my heart, my soul, my mind,
Toward the peace that I can find.
With every step, I'll trust in You,
For Your grace makes all things new.
Help me leave the pain behind,
With hope and joy to fill my mind.
Amen.

A Prayer for Calm in Fearful Times

Lord, my heart is gripped with fear,
Help me feel Your presence near.
When anxious thoughts begin to rise,
Calm me with Your loving eyes.
Replace the fear with perfect peace,
Let all my restless worries cease.
Teach me trust in Your great plan,
Hold me steady in Your hand.
Though storms around me may persist,
I find my refuge in Your midst.
Help me face each fear with grace,
Knowing I am held in Your embrace.
Amen.

Finding Strength in Anxiety

God, I feel weak, my heart unsure,
Help me find strength in You, secure.
When fears arise and cloud my way,
Guide me toward Your light today.
Grant me courage to stand and fight,
Knowing You will make things right.
Let my trust grow strong and true,
For I know I'm safe in You.
In moments when my thoughts run wild,
Calm me with Your peace so mild.
Through You, Lord, I'll rise above,
Held steady by Your endless love.
Amen.

Overcoming the Weight of Fear

Lord, fear has settled in my mind,
Its grip relentless, cruel, unkind.
Help me break free, to rise above,
Held by Your unshakable love.
Replace the worry with steadfast grace,
Help me find a peaceful place.
Guide my thoughts to rest in You,
To trust in all You'll see me through.
You are my rock, my shelter, my shield,
To Your great strength, my fears must yield.
Through every trial, You'll make me whole,
Restoring calm within my soul.
Amen.

A Prayer for Courage in Uncertainty

God, when life feels unsure and strange,
Help me trust You never change.
When fear clouds my heart with doubt,
Clear the way, and lead me out.
Grant me courage to take each step,
Knowing You're here, my soul is kept.
When anxious whispers fill my ears,
Replace them with Your voice that cheers.
Help me stand and face my fear,
With faith that You are always near.
With Your peace, I can embrace,
The challenges ahead with grace.
Amen.

Releasing Anxiety to God

Lord, I surrender my anxious heart,
To You, I give each troubled part.
Take the fears that weigh me down,
Replace them with Your heavenly crown.
Teach me trust and let me see,
Your love has always cared for me.
Help me breathe and rest assured,
Your power and peace are my reward.
When fear creeps in, Lord, hold me tight,
And guide me through the darkest night.
With You, anxiety fades away,
Replaced by peace that's here to stay.
Amen.

Facing the Shadows of Fear

Lord, fear feels like a shadow tall,
Threatening to overtake it all.
But in Your light, shadows retreat,
And fear is trampled beneath Your feet.
Help me trust You're always there,
To lift my burdens, ease my care.
Through every trial, You're my guide,
A steady hand, a place to hide.
When anxious thoughts seek to remain,
Fill me with peace to soothe the strain.
With You, Lord, I can stand strong,
For in Your love, I do belong.
Amen.

Finding Peace in the Storm

Lord, the storm inside me grows,
Anxiety rises, fear overflows.
Speak Your peace into my heart,
And let this anxious storm depart.
Guide me to rest in Your embrace,
To find my courage through Your grace.
Help me breathe through every fear,
Knowing, Lord, that You are near.
Through every wave, my anchor stay,
Your love will guide me through the fray.
In You, my peace is strong and true,
For I am always held by You.
Amen.

A Prayer for Freedom from Fear

God, fear feels like a heavy chain,
Weighing my heart with endless strain.
Break the bonds, set me free,
To live the life You planned for me.
Let Your peace take root inside,
With faith in You as my guide.
Replace each worry, doubt, and fear,
With the truth that You are always near.
Teach me to trust in Your control,
To release the burdens of my soul.
With You, Lord, I am made new,
And fear can never bind me through.
Amen.

Standing Firm in Faith

Lord, when fear makes me hesitate,
Help me walk with courage straight.
When anxiety makes my steps unsure,
Grant me faith that will endure.
Let Your presence fill my mind,
Peace replacing fears unkind.
Help me trust You're by my side,
With every step, as my guide.
Through Your strength, I'll boldly go,
Facing fears that seek to grow.
In Your light, no darkness stays,
For courage fills me all my days.
Amen.

Finding Rest in God's Peace

Lord, I long for peace of mind,
Help me leave my fears behind.
Calm the worry, quiet the strain,
Let Your love flow like healing rain.
When I feel weak, Lord, make me strong,
To face the fears I've carried so long.
Let my heart find rest in You,
For Your promises are always true.
Help me breathe and trust each day,
That Your peace will light my way.
With You, Lord, I am secure,
For Your love will always endure.
Amen.

A Prayer for Divine Inspiration

Lord, my mind feels quiet and still,
Awaiting the spark of Your creative will.
Guide my thoughts, expand my view,
Let inspiration flow through You.
Open my heart to new ideas,
To break free from doubt and hidden fears.
Fill my hands with work of worth,
To bring Your beauty into the earth.
Help me see with clearer sight,
And create with passion, pure and bright.
Through Your Spirit, my soul ignite,
To craft with wisdom and delight.
Amen.

For Creative Vision

God, grant me vision, bold and clear,
To see the wonders You hold near.
Inspire my heart, let ideas take flight,
And guide me with Your holy light.
Help me embrace what I don't yet see,
With courage to shape new creativity.
Let my work reflect Your design,
Unique, authentic, wholly divine.
Through You, Lord, my thoughts align,
With clarity of purpose, both Yours and mine.
In every stroke, every crafted word,
May Your truth and beauty be heard.
Amen.

Unlocking My Creative Flow

Lord, unlock the flow within,
Help my creative work begin.
Free my mind from fear and doubt,
Let inspiration come pouring out.
With each idea, help me explore,
The depths of meaning, and so much more.
Let fresh perspectives fill my mind,
To create with purpose, pure and kind.
Through challenges, help me persevere,
And trust in You to keep me clear.
In every project, large or small,
May Your presence guide it all.
Amen.

A Prayer for Fresh Ideas

God, I need a spark today,
To think anew, to find my way.
Send me ideas, fresh and new,
With insight that reflects You.
Clear the blocks within my mind,
Help me seek and help me find.
Guide my work with steady grace,
And let Your light fill every space.
Grant me courage to take a chance,
To let my creativity dance.
In each step, may Your love show,
Through all the work my hands bestow.
Amen.

For Clarity and Inspiration

Lord, bring clarity to my thought,
Inspire the ideas I have sought.
Open my mind to paths unseen,
To create with purpose, pure and clean.
Let my hands be tools of grace,
Crafting beauty in every space.
With wisdom, Lord, guide my heart,
To see the whole and not just part.
When I feel stuck, renew my view,
To find creative breakthroughs through You.
May all my work be bold and true,
Inspired fully, Lord, by You.
Amen.

A Prayer for Creativity in Challenges

God, when problems seem too vast,
Grant me insight to think fast.
Help me see the hidden way,
Where solutions wait in bright array.
Guide my thoughts with wisdom's hand,
And let me see where You command.
Help me think beyond the norm,
To find new patterns, ideas to form.
With each challenge, let me grow,
With insight only You can show.
In creativity, may I be free,
To reflect Your glory endlessly.
Amen.

Embracing the Creative Spirit

Lord, You are the artist divine,
Help me see Your work in mine.
Fill my heart with creative fire,
To craft and build what You inspire.
Let each stroke, each word I write,
Reflect Your truth, pure and bright.
Help me see the beauty here,
And create with joy, unbound by fear.
Through Your Spirit, make me bold,
To turn ideas into gold.
With gratitude, I lift my hands,
To craft the work Your love commands.
Amen.

A Prayer for Breakthrough Ideas

God, I feel the need for more,
To open wide a creative door.
Help me see beyond my sight,
To find the treasures hidden bright.
Guide my thoughts to innovate,
To find ideas that resonate.
Let me think outside the frame,
To see the world not quite the same.
In every spark, let courage grow,
To shape and form what You bestow.
Through Your wisdom, help me see,
The breakthroughs waiting inside me.
Amen.

For Creativity in Collaboration

Lord, in teamwork, let me shine,
With insights blessed by love divine.
Help me share and also learn,
As creative sparks begin to burn.
Guide our thoughts, unite our hands,
Help us craft what Your love commands.
In each idea, let harmony flow,
To build together and let beauty grow.
May we honour each voice and skill,
With hearts aligned to do Your will.
Through collaboration, let us see,
Your creative hand in unity.
Amen.

Trusting God's Creative Power

God, You are the source of all,
Of every spark, both big and small.
Help me trust Your creative power,
To guide me through each passing hour.
When ideas feel just out of reach,
Inspire me with what You teach.
Let me create with joyful heart,
And trust in You for every part.
In challenges, let me find,
Fresh solutions to ease my mind.
Through all my work, may it be clear,
That Your creativity brought me here.
Amen.

A Prayer for Inner Strength

Lord, the storm inside me grows,
Its weight is heavy, its force it shows.
Help me stand in Your embrace,
With calm and strength, steady my pace.
Through winds of doubt, hold me still,
Align my heart to trust Your will.
When confusion clouds my way,
Shine Your light to lead the day.
Teach me resilience, strong and sure,
To face these trials and endure.
With You, Lord, I will not fall,
Your love sustains me through it all.
Amen.

Finding Calm in the Chaos

God, the chaos surrounds my soul,
Threatening to take control.
Speak Your peace into this storm,
Help me find my steady form.
Though fears may rise and courage wane,
Fill me with strength to bear the strain.
Help me focus, trust, and see,
That Your hand always steadies me.
Through every trial, let me find,
A calm and steadfast state of mind.
In You, Lord, I'm never alone,
You are my shelter, my cornerstone.
Amen.

Strength Amidst Emotional Turmoil

Lord, when emotions overwhelm,
Be my anchor, take the helm.
Guide me through this churning sea,
And help me face what I cannot flee.
Though feelings rage and tears may fall,
Your strength and peace will conquer all.
Teach me to breathe, to trust, to stand,
Held securely in Your hand.
Grant me patience, let me grow,
Through every trial, let wisdom show.
In storms of heart, Your calm instil,
With steadfast faith and unshaken will.
Amen.

A Prayer for Clarity in Confusion

Lord, my mind feels lost and unclear,
Guide my thoughts, draw me near.
When confusion clouds my view,
Help me trust in all You do.
Let resilience grow in my soul,
To rise above and reach my goal.
When doubt and fear begin to creep,
Fill me with courage that runs deep.
In every challenge, make me strong,
To face the chaos and move along.
With You, Lord, I will not break,
Your strength sustains with every step I take.
Amen.

Standing Strong in Crisis

God, in crisis, You are my rock,
My refuge firm against the shock.
When troubles rise and shake my core,
Help me stand, unshaken, sure.
Grant me focus to see the way,
And courage to face another day.
When fear and panic try to bind,
Let peace and wisdom fill my mind.
Teach me patience, let hope abide,
To weather storms with You as my guide.
Through every trial, I'll find my song,
For in Your love, I'm always strong.
Amen.

Finding Peace in Emotional Storms

Lord, emotions swirl and toss,
I feel the weight, I feel the loss.
Help me find a quiet shore,
Where peace resides forevermore.
Through anger, sorrow, fear, and pain,
Guide me back to You again.
Teach me to pause, to breathe, to pray,
To trust You'll lead me through this day.
In Your strength, let me abide,
With steady hands and faith as my guide.
Though storms may rage and trials come,
With You, Lord, I am never undone.
Amen.

Resilience in the Face of Fear

God, fear seeks to pull me down,
To drown me in its chilling sound.
But You are stronger, steadfast, true,
Help me rise and trust in You.
Grant me courage to take each step,
Through darkest nights, my soul is kept.
With every breath, let calmness grow,
In Your presence, let peace flow.
Through trials fierce, I will stand tall,
With faith in You, I'll face it all.
When storms arise, I will not break,
For You are with me, for Your sake.
Amen.

A Prayer for Strength and Hope

Lord, my strength feels small today,
Help me trust in Your steady way.
When life feels heavy, burdens vast,
Let my faith in You hold fast.
Fill my heart with hope anew,
And courage strong to see it through.
When the storm rages, let me find,
Your guiding hand, Your peace of mind.
Teach me to bend, but not to break,
To trust in paths that You will make.
Through every trial, let love remain,
To lift my spirit beyond the pain.
Amen.

Remaining Steadfast in Turmoil

God, in turmoil, I feel weak,
But in Your strength, I will seek.
Hold me firm when life seems hard,
Be my shelter, my strong guard.
Help me endure each wave and blow,
And through it all, let wisdom grow.
When I feel lost, remind me still,
Your steady hand sustains my will.
Teach me patience, help me breathe,
To let Your peace within me seethe.
In every storm, I'll find my ground,
For in Your love, my strength is found.
Amen.

A Prayer for Unshakable Resilience

Lord, the storms of life rage high,
Help me keep my spirit dry.
When doubts and fears shake my core,
Remind me of Your love once more.
Grant me courage, make me bold,
To face each trial, to take hold.
With steadfast faith, help me prevail,
Knowing Your promises never fail.
Through confusion, sorrow, loss, or pain,
I trust in You to lead again.
With You, Lord, I will remain,
Resilient through each trial and strain.
Amen.

Embracing Myself as God's Creation

Lord, You made me as I am,
Designed by Your loving hand.
Help me see the beauty You see,
A reflection of Your divinity.
Teach me to love my imperfections,
To trust in Your perfect intentions.
Silence the voice of harsh critique,
Replace it with truth, tender and unique.
Let me walk with confidence true,
Knowing I am deeply loved by You.
Grant me peace within my soul,
Help me see I am whole.
Amen.

Letting Go of Self-Judgment

God, I am my harshest judge,
My heart is burdened by a heavy grudge.
Help me release the weight of shame,
To see myself as more than blame.
Your love redeems, Your grace restores,
My spirit's worth, forever Yours.
Let self-criticism fade away,
Replaced with hope and love each day.
Teach me kindness for myself,
To value my soul's unique wealth.
In Your light, I am enough,
Accepted, loved, and worthy of trust.
Amen.

Finding Worth in God's Love

Lord, remind me of my worth,
How You've cherished me since birth.
Through Your eyes, I long to see,
The person You created me to be.
Erase the lies that say I'm flawed,
Help me trust I'm loved by God.
Let me embrace my tender heart,
And trust in all You've set apart.
Help me forgive my every fall,
Knowing Your grace redeems it all.
Through Your love, I find my peace,
In self-acceptance, my doubts release.
Amen.

Loving Myself as You Love Me

God, You love me without condition,
Help me see myself with the same vision.
Teach me grace for my mistakes,
And courage for the steps I take.
In Your arms, I'm whole and free,
Help me love the person You see.
Erase the doubt, the fear, the shame,
Remind me, Lord, I bear Your name.
With each breath, let me know,
Self-love helps my spirit grow.
Through You, I find the peace I crave,
A heart redeemed, a soul You save.
Amen.

Breaking Free from Self-Criticism

Lord, self-criticism binds my heart,
Tearing my spirit, keeping us apart.
Help me break these chains of disdain,
To see myself through love again.
You made me whole, a work of art,
With purpose planted in my heart.
Let me honour who I am,
A child of God, redeemed by the Lamb.
Help me celebrate my life, my soul,
To cherish the ways I am made whole.
Through self-love, may I see,
A reflection of Your love for me.
Amen.

For Peace Within Myself

God, my heart is full of doubt,
Show me what Your love's about.
Help me rest in who I am,
Beloved, cherished by the Lamb.
Quiet the voice of cruel despair,
Help me see Your image there.
Teach me to walk with quiet pride,
With You, my worth is verified.
Let me accept my scars and flaws,
Knowing they serve Your holy cause.
Through Your love, I'll find release,
A soul renewed, filled with peace.
Amen.

Forgiving Myself

Lord, I've struggled to forgive myself,
Placing my failures on a shelf.
Help me release the guilt I bear,
To trust Your mercy everywhere.
Teach me to see the good in me,
And how Your grace has set me free.
Let me love myself as You do,
To see my life from a clearer view.
Help me forgive, and let it be,
A step toward loving what You see.
Through Your grace, my heart is new,
Accepting myself as loved by You.
Amen.

Building Confidence in Your Truth

God, my confidence feels so small,
Help me see I'm enough for it all.
Strengthen my heart, my hands, my soul,
Help me see myself as whole.
Let me walk with courage each day,
Trusting the truth You have to say.
Erase the doubts that cloud my mind,
Help me leave self-hate behind.
In Your love, I stand secure,
Through Your grace, I will endure.
Teach me to love myself with care,
For I am Yours, beyond compare.
Amen.

Loving Myself Through Grace

Lord, Your grace is vast and true,
Teach me to give myself grace too.
For every flaw, for every fall,
Remind me, Lord, You've redeemed it all.
Help me to love without regret,
My life, my heart, though imperfect yet.
Let me honour the gifts You've given,
And walk in peace, truly forgiven.
Through Your Spirit, let me grow,
To see the worth You always show.
In self-acceptance, I find release,
A life of joy, a heart at peace.
Amen.

Becoming Whole in Self-Love

God, I long to feel complete,
To love myself as whole, not defeat.
Teach me kindness toward my soul,
To find the beauty in being whole.
Let me see my scars as strength,
A sign of how I've come this length.
Replace my doubts with truth divine,
A heart that's Yours, forever mine.
In self-love, I'll walk each day,
Trusting the words You have to say.
Through You, I find my perfect worth,
Redeemed by love, renewed in birth.
Amen.

A Prayer for Guidance and Wisdom

Lord, I seek Your guiding hand,
To understand what You have planned.
My heart is open, my mind unclear,
Help me see Your presence near.
Reveal the purpose You've designed,
Align my soul, renew my mind.
Through Your wisdom, let me find,
The path of truth, both kind and blind.
Teach me patience, help me hear,
Your whispers soft, Your voice so clear.
In Your light, I long to stay,
To walk with You, my trusted way.
Amen.

Seeking Clarity in Life's Purpose

God, my heart longs to understand,
The mysteries held within Your hand.
What is my purpose, my path, my role?
Guide me, Lord, and make me whole.
Grant me insight, fresh and clear,
To see the reason You've placed me here.
Help me trust in what You show,
And follow boldly where You go.
In moments of doubt, help me stay,
In Your presence, light my way.
Through Your wisdom, I am free,
To live the life You've called for me.
Amen.

A Prayer for Connection to Divine Truth

Lord, I seek a deeper tie,
To see my life through Your great eye.
Grant me the wisdom to comprehend,
The truths You whisper and messages send.
Help me rise beyond the haze,
To see my path through holy ways.
Teach me to trust, to lean, to know,
Your guidance flows where I must go.
With clarity, help me embrace,
The divine purpose You've set in place.
Through love and trust, may I remain,
Connected deeply to Your domain.
Amen.

Disclaimer

This book, Prayers for Mental Clarity, is intended to offer spiritual support, encouragement, and reflection. It is not a substitute for professional mental health care, medical treatment, or counselling. If you are experiencing mental health challenges, stress, anxiety, or any other condition that may require medical or psychological intervention, please consult a licensed healthcare professional.

The prayers and reflections in this book are not designed to diagnose, treat, cure, or prevent any medical condition. Rather, they are meant to provide comfort, spiritual insight, and an opportunity for personal growth. Each person's spiritual journey is unique, and the contents of this book are offered as a resource to support you in your path toward mental clarity and inner peace.

The author and publisher disclaim any liability arising from the use or misuse of the information in this book. Readers are encouraged to use these prayers as part of a balanced approach to wellness, including professional guidance when needed.